Uncle Foster's Hat Tree

by Doug Cushman

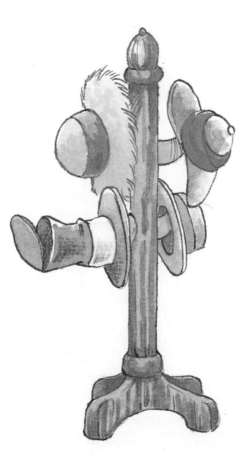

PUFFIN BOOKS

for Leonard Everett Fisher

PUFFIN BOOKS
Published by the Penguin Group
Penguin Books USA Inc., 375 Hudson Street, New York, New York 10014, U.S.A.
Penguin Books Ltd, 27 Wrights Lane, London W8 5TZ, England
Penguin Books Australia Ltd, Ringwood, Victoria, Australia
Penguin Books Canada Ltd, 10 Alcorn Avenue, Toronto, Ontario, Canada M4V 3B2
Penguin Books (N.Z.) Ltd, 182–190 Wairau Road, Auckland 10, New Zealand

Penguin Books Ltd, Registered Offices: Harmondsworth, Middlesex, England

First published in the United States of America by E. P. Dutton,
a division of NAL Penguin, 1988
Published simultaneously in Canada by Fitzhenry & Whiteside Limited, Toronto
Published in a Puffin Easy-to-Read edition, 1996

5 7 9 10 8 6

The Library of Congress has cataloged the Dutton edition as follows:
Cushman, Doug.
Uncle Foster's hat tree.

Summary: Merle hears four entertaining stories about the hats
on Uncle Foster's hat tree and then gets to try on the hats.
[1. Hats—Fiction.] I. Title.
PZ7.C959Un   1988   [E]   88-3573
ISBN 0-525-44410-6

Puffin Easy-to-Read ISBN 0-14-03.7995-9

Printed in the United States of America

Reading Level 1.8

Contents

It was raining.

Merle was stuck

at Uncle Foster's house.

There was nothing to do.

He was bored.

"Look around the house,"

said Uncle Foster.

"Okay," said Merle.

He found something strange

in the hall.

"What is that?" asked Merle.

"That is a hat tree,"

Uncle Foster said.

"And those are my hats.

There is a story

about each hat.

Sit down and I will tell you."

Uncle Foster's Jungle Hat

I was in the jungle.

We were looking for dinosaur bones.

I heard my friend yell,

"Foster! Come quickly!"

He was down in a deep hole.

"Look!" he said.

"I found the bones

of a rare dinosaur."

We had to get

them to the museum.

"You stay here," I cried,

"I will tell the museum."

We were far away from the village.

The only way to get there was by boat.

I ran to the river

and pushed the boat in.

I began to row

to the village.

The boat bumped into a log.

I took my oar

and began to poke it.

The log opened its eyes.

Then it grinned.

It wasn't a log at all.

It was a crocodile!

I rowed and rowed.

The crocodile swam and swam.

My arms were very tired.

I had to slow down.

The crocodile caught up with me.

He opened his mouth.

CHOMP!

He took a big bite of my boat.

It began to sink.

I thought fast.

I still had the oar.

So I took my hat off

and turned it upside down.

There was just enough room

to sit inside.

I began to row.

14

The hat was light.

I went very fast.

The crocodile was left way behind me.

I made it to the village

and called the museum.

The dinosaur arrived safely

soon after.

No bones about that!

Uncle Foster's Garden Hat

"What is that hat?" Merle asked.

"That is my garden hat,"

Uncle Foster said.

"It is old now.

But I remember

when it was brand-new."

I was out in the garden.

It was very hot.

I took off my hat

and laid it on the ground.

Then I went to the shed

for my hoe.

When I returned, my hat was gone!

Where could it have gone?

I looked in the garden.

I looked in the street.

I looked in the bushes.

But no hat.

I scratched my head

and looked up.

There was my hat!

It was in the tree!

I began to climb.

Then my hat began to move.

It jumped. It jiggled.

Two baby birds popped up over the brim.

"*Tweet,*" they cried.

"*Tweet, tweet.*"

23

My hat was now a nest.

If I took my hat back,

where would the birds live?

I went inside to think.

I came out later with lots

of old hats.

"Take any old hat you want,"

I told the birds.

"I just want my new hat back."

25

The birds took the old hats.

I climbed up the tree

to get my new hat.

The baby birds

were in a new old hat.

Everyone now had a hat

and a home.

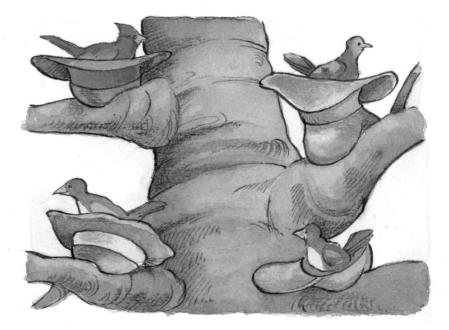

Uncle Foster's Straw Hat

"I was in show business once,"

Uncle Foster said.

"I wore this straw hat."

I had an act with a friend.

We sang and danced

and told jokes.

Then at the end of the act

we threw whipped-cream pies.

That always got a big laugh.

Then we passed a hat.

People tossed money in.

One day,

in with all the money

there was a note.

If he liked us,

The governor would pay us well.

But he was a grumpy man.

He hardly ever smiled.

We were scared.

That night the governor sat

in the front row.

We danced our best dances.

We sang our best songs.

We told our best jokes.

Everyone loved us.

But the governor never smiled.

Then we began to throw

our whipped-cream pies.

I was so excited.

I threw my pie too hard.

It flew through the air.

SMACK! Right in the governor's face.

The room became silent.

No one laughed

or made a sound.

The governor got up

and walked onto the stage.

He looked mad.

"That is no way

to throw a pie," he said.

"Do it like this!"

And he threw a pie at me.

33

He burst out laughing.

"I used to be

in show business too,"

he said.

"And we threw pies

at the end of *our* act."

He threw a pie at his wife.

She threw one at him.

I threw a pie back.

Soon the whole room was

a mountain of whipped cream.

35

The governor put

lots of money in this hat.

There was also a note.

It was his own recipe

for whipped-cream pie.

Uncle Foster's Top Hat

"This is my top hat,"

Uncle Foster said.

"I wore it to a grand ball."

We all dressed

in our best clothes.

We rode in a fine carriage.

Suddenly the carriage stopped.

A voice cried,

"Everyone out! Hands up!"

We were being robbed!

The robber took

our money and jewels.

"That is a fine hat,"

he said to me.

"Hand it over."

The robber put it on.

"That is not the way

to wear a top hat,"

I said.

"Wear it lower."

"Like this?" the robber asked.

"Let me help," I said.

I pulled the hat down

over his head and shoulders.

"Like this!" I cried.

He couldn't move.

We took him to jail.

"You are very brave,"

the sheriff said.

"My hat is off to you."

Uncle Foster Tips His Hat

"Those were good stories,"

Merle said.

"Can I try on some of the hats?"

"Let's try them all on,"

Uncle Foster said.

44

He went to the window.

"Look! The rain has stopped,"

he said.

"Let's go outside."

The clouds had moved away.

The moon was shining.

"Can you see

the Man in the Moon?"

Uncle Foster asked.

"Yes," Merle said.

"He looks like he is waving.

Should we wave back?"

"Let's tip our hats,"

said Uncle Foster.

So they did.